THE PACIFIC CREST TALES

Hiking and Reverence

Circa the Post-Pandemic 2020s—

The Current Post-Plague Medieval Era

John Ostrander

Pacific Crest Trail
Association

Campsite just south of the Goat Rocks, at approximately mile 2255 north from the Mexican border. Artist: James Ostrander.

• Prologue •

When come July with showers past,
the days long and the nights short,
then longen folk to go on pilgrimage.
South to North, through the Sierra
and into Cascadia, on the path of the
Pacific Crest. The most devout, the
"through hikers," walk for months
from Mexico to Canada, usually
twenty to thirty miles each day—
at times together, at times apart, at
times in parley, at times in silence.

In the evening, sundry folk by
adventure and chance assemble at
places randomly found along the
trail, level for sleep near water
fresh, seeking fellowship and rest.
After setting up tents, preparing and
eating meals, nearby hikers often
gather with hiker friends, "trail

families," and newly met hikers. Per trail custom, they had bestowed "trail names" upon one another during their journey.

This night, at an opening in the conifer canopy, under clear and balmy heavens, the following pilgrims found themselves together: Songbird (pretty and lithe, wearing a "Santa Monica track club" tank top over deeply tanned arms), Sir Lancelot (sturdy and tall, but couldn't hardly grow a beard), Repo Man (wearing a faded Bob Marley T-shirt that said "Don't Worry about a Thing," matching his sense of self) and Unicorn (a truly unique fellow, a pantomath, who looked like a conventional painting of Jesus—long, dark hair; a full beard; kind, expressive eyes—if Jesus also had a backpack and muscled soccer player legs). As the night advanced, they were joined by three more: Hoot (a reserved, light-sleeping British Indian woman), Shredder (a tall, athletic Midwesterner, wearing a batik-print skirt over dusty beat-up hiking boots), and John Doe (freakishly athletic and new to most of the others). Tales and fellowship were shared.

• Songbird's Tale •

Songbird was freshly returned to the trail after a brief break when she hitched to the town of Randall, Washington—a logging town in spirit, if less so now in fact. Songbird loved to talk, and she loved the trail camaraderie. She thrived in the vastness of untamed nature, uncrowded by career counselors, corporate micro-managers, and the rest of the advancement and expectation ilk. This evening, like many evenings in the past, she happily began the story telling.

"I had just finished a 24-hour challenge, and during the last twenty miles, I was thinking *ONLY* about a big greasy hamburger with onion rings. You know, heart attack on a bun. I was famished. More famished than tired, even. So, when I reached the highway, early afternoon, I hitched a ride. Easy for me to do—single blonde girl on an empty highway. I had barely gone ten miles when I saw a bar advertising 'Best Burger in the Pacific Northwest,' so I told my ride, a friendly trucker dude, to stop.

"It took a while for my eyes to adjust to the dark inside, but it was a typical logger, or ex-logger, bar: pool tables, Coors Light neon, a couple big fellows at the bar starting in heavy though it wasn't yet 2:00 p.m. (it had to be 5:00 pm somewhere). A refuge of the hidden and hiding.

"The bartender, a bear man with a beard that would make a nice nest for a family of mice, smiled. But it was one of those 'well, well, well, little girl' smiles that I totally hate. When he asked, 'What would you like, Miss?' I told him I wanted the biggest hamburger he could make.

"Bear Man scoffed, telling me that would be the Fat Bottom *Dee-Lux* burger, but decided that I couldn't eat it all. He pointed to the two big guys at the bar, who he said couldn't eat one even though they were about three times my size. He then called me 'little lady,' which really pissed me off, and said that he'd make me a regular, promising it'd be ready 'in a jiff.' Can you believe that shit?"

"So, what did you do?" asked Sir Lancelot.

Songbird smiled impishly. "Of course, I ordered the Fat Bottom *Dee-Lux* burger with extra onion rings on the side.

"And, it was BIG, filling the entire plate. It had six strips of bacon, onions, lettuce, tomato, and some gooey pink sauce. I truly hadn't ever seen such a big burger. It was so huge . . . it took me some time . . . to eat *all* of it . . . *and* to scarf down the rings."

"Good job! What did Bear Man say?" asked Repo Man.

"Oh, he and the others were talkin' smack when it came out. You know, 'lil' bigger than you thought, Missy?' All that sexual innuendo bullshit joke shit—a bunch of fucking arrested-development juveniles. You know, like 'she didn't realize how big it was, har, har, har'—as if their burger was their penis size." Sir Lancelot blushed. "But they shut the fuck up as I ate it. Every single bite. They had no clue about what a hungry PCT girl can do!"

Hearty cheers by all.

"Right on! What happened next?" asked Repo Man.

"Oh, this is the best part. I looked Bear Man right in the eye, and said, 'You know, you were right.' He was the sort that desperately needs to be right even about the puniest things. So, I leaned over and said to him, 'Yeah, you were right about having the regular burger.' He started to regain his smug look. I then said, 'So . . . I think I will *also* have one of those *regular* hamburgers. And throw in some fries with it. Can you get that to me in a jiff?' You should've seen their faces! The three of them! It was a thing of beauty! I rattled a few gender stereotypes there. The second burger tasted pretty good too, but I was both pretty full and ready to crash hard—so it was really tough for me to finish the second one off."

Big smiles all around.

Sensing that prim Sir Lancelot might have been made uncomfortable by her brashness toward Bear Man, Songbird turned toward him and said, "As I left, I told Bear Man that he made about the best damn burgers I've ever tasted, and I'd be sure to tell all my starving hiking buds. He liked that, so we're all good."

• Sir Lancelot's Tale •

Sir Lancelot may have been the tidiest through hiker on the entire PCT. He was a modern knight if there ever was one. (Okay, he was just a big boy scout, lovable and dorky, but he was trying, and it was charming in a youthful, awkward way.)

Sir Lancelot earnestly wanted to be perceived as a worthy man—a devotee of honor and courtesy. Living per his own created code of proper conduct was important to him, and if it at first seemed artificial, it was so genuinely felt that he was generally liked. His backpack was heavier than most, laden with extra safety equipment that would never be used. He was smitten with Songbird in a chaste and wholesome manner. But he was clueless. Unaware that he never had a chance.

Sir Lancelot warned Songbird about hitchhiking, and offered to accompany her the next time she needed a ride because "very strange things can happen."

"Thanks," Songbird said, "but I can handle myself

. . . probably better than you can. Besides, no offense, but no one would pick me up with you in tow."

Sir Lancelot, undeterred, continued, "Well, there are some strange people around. Where the trail crosses Highway 12 at White Pass, the road to Randall where you hitched, I came across a real character . . . I'll call him 'Mr. Miller.'

"Mr. Miller was intoxicated. Very intoxicated. He was only about a hundred yards down the trail off the highway when we literally ran into each other around a corner. Mr. Miller would have fallen if I hadn't braced him. He said he was looking for a 'libtard or two' because he had 'some things to tell 'em.' I told him that he might not have much luck on the trail, as politics seemed pretty remote out here. I am a political moderate, and maybe even bordering on conservative, at least on certain issues.

Mr. Miller then got a funny, puzzled look on his face. He suddenly turned greenish and started throwing up. Reflexively, he grabbed his ball cap, and, holding the brim, tried mostly unsuccessfully to catch his vomit in the cap. He was *so* intoxicated. When I yelled, 'Your hat isn't a bucket,' he grunted, 'Oh, thanks,' *and put it back on his head!*"

"Gross!" said Songbird.

"Niiice!" said Repo Man.

"Well, it was disgusting," continued Sir Lancelot. "He was standing there with a trickle of vomit oozing down his cheek. He never told me his name, but his cap had a 'Miller Highlife' decal. Hence, 'Mr. Miller.'"

"Love that Miller 'Girl in the Moon,' toasting life and the stars," said Unicorn.

Sir Lancelot glanced quizzically at Unicorn before continuing.

"I escorted Mr. Miller back to the road, where he insisted on resting. While I was considering next steps, he sprawled out and suddenly started snoring, sawing logs. I figured it was safest for everyone to just allow him to sleep it off."

Sir Lancelot then rolled into a general pseudo-advisory message about how merely one mile from the trailhead is officially deemed to be "wilderness," meaning that one needs to carry proper safety equipment, which he started to list off. "Bear spray, a whistle ..."

The others let Lance go on for a bit because the 'Mr. Miller' story had been a laugh. But eventually, interest started to lag, and Repo Man gently interrupted.

"You make great points," he said, "but you're talking to some pretty experienced hikers who've all been on the trail for months. My guess is that we've got the safety stuff down. We're just chillin', tellin' tales now."

Looking around sheepishly, Sir Lancelot grimaced. "Oh yeah, I guess you're right. That last bit wasn't really a story. But I have another story. A *real* story."

Seeking not to lose the earlier good mood, and looking for a fresh voice, Unicorn piped up.

"I feel in my bones that Repo Man probably has a hell of a story to tell us."

Sir Lancelot, like everyone, was fond of Repo Man, and willingly turned to listen to him. Any resentments he felt at being shut down were directed at Unicorn, whom Sir Lancelot never really cared for.

• Repo Man's Tale •

Repo Man had worked one summer for a tow-truck company, but that had nothing to do with his trail name. That came from his proud claim to be from "E-Po Portland," meaning East Portland. Another hiker had thought he said "Repo-land," which led to a hilariously ironic trail name. Unlike a cold-hearted bill collector, Repo Man exuded a nice, easy manner, was very kind, and had a constant gentle smile.

"I guess I do have a story," Repo Man said. "Or at least a mystery about my Uncle Carey. I'm still trying to figure it all out. I don't know where to start."

"Who's your Uncle Carey?" asked Songbird.

"Well, that's just it. I don't really know. It's crazy, and he's a crazy dude."

"Crazy how?" asked Songbird and Sir Lancelot in unison.

"Well, he would deliver mystery gifts, write mystery letters, and pretty much appear or disappear from my life like a ghost."

"Ooh, now you got us interested. What kinda gifts are you talking about?" asked Unicorn.

"Well, the first gift I remember was when I turned six or seven. Carey gave me a .22 rifle. That may be kinda normal in some places, but *not* in our E-Po village. It's a no-guns, hate-free, rainbow neighborhood full of fringe activists and fried hippies. When I opened my present at a block party, the villagers gasped in horror, as if I'd unwrapped a decapitated head. I don't remember my parents' reaction, but I imagine they just shrugged and dismissed it as typical Uncle Carey behavior." Repo Man paused nostalgically. "But, unlike my friends, I learned to shoot."

"What else did he give you?" asked Songbird.

"Okay, get this . . . right before prom, I was feeling a little jittery. I was unsure about the whole prom deal, and suddenly UPS delivers a package with a dried leathery cup tied to a string, which I later learned was a *saco de toro*. There was also a note that said, 'Just have fun, be nice, and be glad you aren't this guy.'"

"What'd he give you? A sacko—what was that called?" asked Sir Lancelot.

"*Saco de toro*. A bull's sack or scrotum. Cut off and dried, hanging on some twine. Its a Spanish thing."

"For prom? That's messed up," said Songbird. "Really funny, but messed up!"

"Was that supposed to be your corsage?" asked Sir Lancelot.

"Chicks wear corsages. Dudes wear boutonnieres. But, no, it wasn't to be worn. It was just a joke and a message. It was a classic Uncle Carey ... or whoever."

Repo Man then tried to explain Uncle Carey—or "Kerry," as it was sometimes written.

"My dad told me that Uncle Carey was my mom's *older* brother, but sometimes he told me that Uncle Carey was my mom's *younger* brother. That's not a big deal. My dad was a great man with grand ideas, but he smoked too much weed and was never good with details. My dad would go off on rants, and to sound like he knew what he was talking about, he'd solemnly cite facts and figures. But the number of war deaths would grow, and other 'facts' became more outrageous when he sensed that no one was paying attention—as often happened when he went on too long. Then my mom would cut him off with a smile, saying something sweet. She was very protective of everyone. She was also the very organized one." Repo Man rubbed his face with both hands and looked around at the others staring intently at him.

"So anyway, here's the mystery. I remember thinking it was odd that my mom always said that Uncle Carey was my *dad's* younger brother. You'd think my parents would know their own siblings."

"Seems pretty basic," remarked Sir Lancelot.

"I was told that Uncle Carey was in the war. After Afghanistan, he didn't return home. I would ask, but no one knew how to get ahold of him. We never saw him, and I don't think I've seen a remotely current picture of him. But somehow he *always* remembered my birthday, and was very timely, thoughtful, and funny in the most unexpected ways."

The others listened intently.

Repo Man continued. "Uncle Carey was like my mother in that he always knew exactly what was needed and just at the right time. But the gifts he sent were not like my mother's. They were out there, edgy—more like something my father would do. As I got older, I wondered if Uncle Carey was real. Maybe he didn't even exist. In my late teens, I had a big revelation—or I thought it was a big revelation. I concluded that 'Uncle Carey' was just a *fiction* created by my parents. No one else could know so much about my life, and care enough to do something for me, and always with perfect 'mom-timing.' I figured that it was all just a long-planned ploy that allowed my parents to do things for me, to teach me, after I naturally would start to resist them."

"That's really pretty clever," observed Songbird. Sir Lancelot readily agreed.

"What did your parents say when you called bullshit on the Uncle Carey ruse?" asked Songbird.

"Well, I never did. My dad got an aggressive cancer. During his final weeks, I heard from Uncle Carey a few times—just small 'check ins' that simply let me know that I had someone caring about me. But at the time, I wasn't thinking about the Carey mystery."

Repo Man's voiced cracked. Songbird put her hand on his shoulder. The other hikers shook their heads sympathetically.

"Three weeks after Dad's memorial, Mom was killed by a drunk driver."

The other hikers responded at once.

"Oh, dear!"

"I'm so sorry."

"That sucks."

"Thanks," Repo Man said. "Yeah, suddenly I was alone and unsure what to do. Life continued in a pretty rough way. A couple weeks later, I lost my job, and my girlfriend dumped me. When I went to my PO Box, I got a notice that my landlord was converting my apartment to condos, giving me sixty days to vacate."

"Oh, dear!" repeated Songbird.

"What trying circumstances," said Sir Lancelot.

"Yet, amazingly, you're this mellow, chill dude," observed Unicorn.

Repo Man shrugged. "I felt completely run over, and totally dazed."

"No doubt." "Jeeeesus!" Songbird and Unicorn spoke at the same time.

"Yeah, after reading my landlord's 'love note,' I almost didn't see a delivery notice amidst the junk mail. I gave it to the postal clerk, who gave me a big package—this fancy US Special Forces backpack." He paused to pat his backpack. "And also this note, which I've been carrying since." Repo Man pulled out a dog-eared piece of paper and read from it.

> Hang in there, buddy. You are unbelievably strong, talented, and good. As I've always told you, there are no problems, only solutions. The PCT is waiting to be hiked.
>
> Love, Uncle Carey

"Holy shit!" said Songbird. "Carey *is* real!"

"So then," Unicorn said, "you ended up hanging with us outcasts on the PCT?"

"Well, yeah. Here I am."

There was silence while the story sunk in.

"Have you heard from him since?"

"Not a word. But lately, I haven't exactly been near a mailbox."

Unicorn exhaled. "Man. That *is* a hell of a story. Hell of a story. So, what's the explanation? Is Carey in the CIA? Mossad? Prison? Witness protection? You gotta have figured this out."

"Uh, what? No. I mean, I don't know. I'm still clueless about Uncle Carey. But on this hike, I've grown comfortable not knowing. Just like happenings on the trail. I'm good with the gray." He paused, and then added, "But I do know this. This hike is one of the best things I've done in my life. I'm thankful to Carey for leading me to it."

"Right on for that!" Unicorn said. "But as for Carey, you have no idea where he is, or even really what he looks like? Wow! Who knows, maybe he'll show up in Portland . . . or maybe we'll run into Carey on the trail!"

"I'd like that! Now that would be some outrageous 'trail magic'!" The hikers kicked back, musing about unrealistic but pleasant thoughts of magical possibilities.

• Hoot •

It was now the end of the golden hour. The sun had set, basking the landscape in the soft summer afterglow of the northern latitudes. Hoot softly entered the camping area.

She was familiar to the others, if not well known. Her trail name came from the fact that when she started hiking, just north of the Mexican border, Hoot was very nervous about snakes. There are no rattlesnakes in London, and she frequently awoke at night keeping watch for reptile intruders. The name also fit because she was quiet and typically perched on the edge of gatherings, silently taking everything in like a wise owl. Occasionally, she'd surprise everyone, swooping in with a trenchant observation or comment that was always spot on.

This evening, Hoot was greeted warmly, but she demurred to inquiries.

"Don't mind me. I'll just sit here on the end for a while. Carry on."

Hoot enjoyed the story telling. She also liked to compare in her mind the stories of others with her own secret and riveting tale. The one that led her to this remote wilderness, far from Southall and the rest of London, and far from *watta satta.*

She had been trying to make sense of her personal plight for hundreds of miles. She felt so comfortable with these hiking pilgrims, these roving trail families, that she occasionally wondered how they would react if she had told them her tale.

Hoot then imagined how that would go. She would describe her older brother Ravi, who at home was perceived as a great success and a matrimonial "catch." But Ravi was cruel. Cruel and dangerous. She could not believe he was her brother. She knew this. She knew it her entire life. As a young child, Ravi would casually torture stray animals. As a teen, he would maliciously hurt anyone he perceived was a competitor or a threat. Yet he could always turn on the charm and evade any serious consequence for his wrongs.

As a young man, Ravi had probably gotten worse. He was at least more devious. On the surface, he presented as an attractive, smooth-talking, wickedly clever young solicitor. But he was still Ravi.

Hoot could not escape him. As brother and sister, Ravi and Hoot were supposed to marry another brother-sister pair. That is *watta satta.* Hoot could not allow Ravi to marry Rowena, who Hoot knew to be kind and gentle. Hoot was also personally afraid of any double union. When Ravi acted like Ravi and hurt Rowena, Hoot expected that she would probably suffer at the hands of Rowena's brother, Rahul. That is the built-in "protection" of *watta satta*. Handle everything within the families. But with Ravi, it just meant that Hoot would pay the price for her brother's sadistic nature. He would like that. Double the pain. There was no escape.

Unless there *was* an escape. Hiking the PCT felt like an escape. It certainly was a reprieve. Here, amidst the wild—so different from England—Hoot was stronger. Physically, of course. But mentally as well. The blimey twists and turns of the trail built up both self-confidence and an inoculation of sorts against pain caused by societal risks. She could not do anything about Ravi, but the problems he caused seemed somewhat more manageable now. Time spent gazing at the awesome milky way at night had given her perspective and mental strength.

And despite temptation, for now Hoot would hold on to her story. The untold stories were too much for most people to handle. Meanwhile, her precious and rare feelings of personal power would continue to grow. She would get stronger.

• Unicorn's Insights and Divinations •

Songbird's cheery voice broke Hoot's reverie. "What about you, Unicorn? Do you have a mystery uncle?"

"I don't have anything crazy like that," he said. "I don't even have a story to tell. But I *have* recently figured out some amazing truths, which've been hidden from at least half of us for like practically ever. And these have been totally blowing my mind for the last 150 miles."

"What are they?" asked Songbird.

"Tell us!" said Repo Man.

"You aren't gonna believe this, but . . ." He paused for dramatic effect. "I've cracked the Angela Code."

"Who's Angela?" asked Songbird.

Unicorn continued, excitedly. "There's lots of Angelas. Some are called Emily, some are called Emma, some are called Chloe, and some are called Angela. And pretty much all women, or people who identify as women, have the Code. But a lot of them don't use their gift, or maybe even don't know they have it. There's a lot I'm still trying to figure out. But there are a couple of giveaways or tells for true self-aware Angelas. For instance, the Apex Angelas always wear turquoise jewelry somewhere. Turquoise seems to be really, really important. They also tend to favor danglees along with nose piercings."

"Whoa, whoa, whoa!" Songbird said, laughing. "I'm totally confused. First, who doesn't like turquoise? And what's this Code that Angela, or a bunch of people have?" asked Songbird.

Unicorn again paused dramatically.

"The Angela Code is the ability to read dudes' minds."

"Really?" Songbird said incredulously between laughter. "That's it? *That's* your big discovery? I'll freely admit that I pretty much got that gift. What do dudes think about? Food and sex. I've also got the gift of reading the minds of golden retrievers: 'Give me the ball, give me the ball, give me the ball. Can I jump in the water? Give me the ball.'"

"True, true. But this isn't just base impulses. Angelas know your thoughts, and even what just briefly crossed your mind. It's like they know your mental search history. And a critical part of the Code is that they don't tell anyone about their powers and what they learn, except other Angelas. Or at least I *think* they tell, or telepathically communicate with, other Angelas."

Getting even more excited, Unicorn continued in a torrent. "This is a *really* big deal. See, cracking the Code helps accelerate humanity's realignment with the natural world at its core, which can unlock evolution to so many things—maybe even a kinder, more supportive form of capitalism and democracy. There's so much more to figure out, but evolutionarily speaking, having the gift and keeping it secret seems to be key. You know, thinking in the form of scheming is the type of thinking that can be passed on from generation to generation. Pure thinking, or the altruistic contemplation of all potential ramifications, is counter to survival in the wild. Those traits get cleaned out by the system. Just look at Socrates . . . Lumumba . . . uh . . . Anne Frank."

"Man, you are losing us," said Repo Man, with a big grin. "Slow down, slow down . . . Lumumba? Really? How did you . . . ah . . . figure this out?"

"Luck. A little help to open my mind, but then I got it. And I confirmed it with an Apex Angela. Her name was Zoey. I had to wait until she was completely mellow and totally zoning with me. You know, like when you just sit there and look at each other and breathe at the same time, and blink at the same time, and I'm sure your hearts beat at the same tempo. When you are in that zone, you are the same person—neither male, female, trans; neither human nor animal. Just two living beings in the same space. We could have been two sea urchins in a Pacific tide pool. And when I asked her to tell me what she saw with her inner eye, she told me. Psilocybin really helped, but then it then *all* started to make sense."

• Two More Hikers •

"Did someone say psilocybin?" asked a female voice coming from two hiker headlights striding quickly toward the campsite. "That must be you, Unicorn!"

The crowd recognized Shredder. She was from the upper Midwest, taking a gap year before grad school at Northwestern. She was sort of a legend on the trail. She typically walked alone at a *very* fast pace, passing all the other through hikers, but lately she had fallen behind the pack when she took a couple of weeks worth of zero days dealing with some family business. Now, she was back outpacing everyone again.

Shredder was enthusiastically welcomed, and she introduced her companion as 'John Doe.' He wore a solid green nylon shirt and was built like an Olympic decathlete. John Doe and Repo Man had identical US Special Forces IOTV backpacks, a rarity on the trail. Against John Doe's absurdly broad shoulders, his backpack looked trifling, almost like the kind a child would wear to school.

"So, Shredder, it looks like you found someone who can keep up with you," said Repo Man warmly. Shredder nodded. "Its all good to walk alone," she said. "But it's a nice change to walk with someone." The new hikers comfortably joined the group.

Unicorn broadly smiled. He was happy to see Shredder. He then started to ramp up again. "Now, Songbird, I love you, and you are wonderful, but tell us. You knew that we'd be joined by Shredder and her Greek God companion, right? *That's the Code.* You know I'm right about Angela powers, but you won't admit it—that's that evolutionary bit, right? But I'm still trying to figure out so many more questions. What is the magic of turquoise? Why do you like it so much? Does it help with the telepathic communication? How does turquoise help with the realignment?"

Before Songbird could answer, and before Unicorn could really get going again, Sir Lancelot, tired of Unicorn, cut in. "I'm sorry to interrupt, but I *do* have a story to share. A *real* story this time!"

The group turned to him, and he began.

• Sir Lancelot's Fable •

"A couple of deer, a rabbit, a skunk, and a crow lived deep in the Oregon woods. They were all headed toward Mt. Hood, away from a bunch of scary 'two-legs,' who were invading their valley. They came together in a clearing in front of an ominous cave emitting a nasty sulphur smell and an eerie gurgling sound. The deer and the rabbit were ready to bolt, as is their nature, but the skunk cautioned that no one should jump to conclusions based on an odor. He said that smelly things tend to keep two-legs away, are actually very nice, and should be respected."

"Skunk's right," injected Unicorn. "Don't dare piss off Goddess Pele. She's passionate, unpredictable and volatile." Familiar with, and fond of, Unicorn's vast knowledge of obscure information, Repo Man and Shredder smiled and exchanged knowing side glances.

Sir Lancelot continued. "The crow added that he had flown high, and confirmed this was still the best route to the mountain, as there were several similar fumaroles all around. The animals respected skunk's wisdom and crow's perspective. Comforted by their unlikely fellowship, they all ventured past the cave together and made it up to the Mt. Hood timberline. In later days, they would on occasion think back to that scary moment and realize that they were better off for having trusted one another, notwithstanding their great differences."

Having told a real story, a fable, Sir Lancelot beamed as he looked around at his audience.

"What a sweet, wholesome story, Lance," said Songbird, affectionately.

"Now *that's* a story!" Repo Man agreed. Then he laughed. "Just so long as you're not calling me a skunk."

"Yes, that *was* sweet," said Shredder. "A classic bedtime story. But if you guys want to hear an intense, true-life tale, you gotta listen to John Doe."

• John Doe's Tale •

"Hey, thanks for letting me join your group," John Doe said. "I'm not much of a talker, but if Shredder likes you, that's fine by me."

"Cool, but what's the deal with the name 'John Doe'?" asked Repo Man.

Shredder answered for him. "People gave him trail names," she said, "but they didn't fit, or they were taken, or . . ."

"Yeah." John Doe cut in. "For a while, I was good with 'Flip Flop.' I like to wear flippies in camp and that seemed innocent enough. But then everyone told me there already was another hiker named Flip Flop doing the trail."

"Oh, yeah! Flip Flop's witty as hell and way cool!" said Repo Man. "You know she's also from Portland."

"Yay, Flip Flop!" added Songbird. "She's very nice! Although I don't much care for her hiking partner, Hermit."

"Anyway," Shredder continued. "Some other names

fit *too* well, and they hit some nerves. It became such a thing that I started calling the big guy, 'John Doe Number 1,' or sometimes 'JDO—John Doe Outlaw.' Those were too much of a mouthful, so now we just use 'John Doe,' which I like, and which has grown on him."

John Doe nodded. "My real name is Franklin, but I trust Shredder, and 'John Doe' is kinda funny. It took about fifty trail miles, but now I'm all good with it. It makes me smile when I hear it. You may not know this, but Shredder is a badass hiker, and the only person that I've met who hikes at my pace."

"We know!" the others said in a chorus of recognition and admiration.

John Doe continued. "I've seen lots of hikers. I've hiked the entire AT, or Appalachian Trail, and the Continental Divide Trails."

"Wow!" said Unicorn. "That's intense."

"It *was* intense, totally intense when I hiked the AT. I hiked that trail angry. See, I'd done some stupid things. Bad things. I got into trouble, but I was given a chance at . . . ah . . . redemption, if I completed the entire AT. I started in Georgia and hiked for 500 miles angry. Angry at everyone. I never talked to the other hikers. I was just doing my task, doing my time, marking miles like marking jail time on a cell wall. I was alone and pissed off."

The others listened with rapt attention.

"Then it came to me. I found that I was actually pretty athletic, and pretty good at this hiking stuff. I still didn't talk to anyone, but I kind of liked hearing people comment, you know, 'Wow, you got legs' and 'We can't keep up with you.' People seemed genuinely nice, which I wasn't used to. By the time I reached Katahdin, pretty much ahead of everyone else, I was in the best shape of my life and hooked on long-distance hiking. I talked to my special guy about it, and he told me about the CD trail. What's more, out of his own pocket, he funded me, so I could keep up what he called the 'good progress.' I pretty much owe everything to my special guy."

John Doe paused and glanced at his audience's friendly receptive faces and continued.

"Deep in Colorado, I really began to understand. I was long done hiking angry. And I stopped hiking just as an athletic feat. I started listening to the birds, the insects, the wind in the trees. It was meditation. Kinetic meditation. I wasn't even walking. I was just part of the landscape. I didn't want anything. I don't need anything. Meeting my base and simple needs while hiking was more satisfying than anything I had ever known. I was truly happy. I was humbled. *I am* humbled. And I am so thankful that I can be here. It is absolutely beautiful here. *So beautiful and awesome.*"

The others vigorously nodded and smiled at John Doe.

"Yeah, you guys get it. You know the Zen or whatever it is. And now, on the PCT, I met Shredder, and I'm now at an even higher level. We don't need to talk. Sometimes we do, but we don't need to. And the people here, like you guys, are all okay. Better than okay. Pretty damn good, actually. Good people fit into the landscape. It just keeps getting more and more . . . awe-inspiring."

This was greeted by the group with more nodding, smiling, and a general aura of good feeling.

"You are preaching the truth, bro," said Repo Man.

"Right on! Al-jihad al-akbar!" said Unicorn triumphantly, to the mildly baffled look of John Doe.

"I've missed you, Unicorn," said Shredder, affectionately. "You are the font of the totally obscure and unexpected."

"You're scary, dude," said Repo Man, looking at Unicorn and smiling broadly. "I don't understand half of what comes out of your mouth, but I'm thinking you know so many bizarre and different things that maybe there's something to *all* the far-out stuff you say!"

Then Repo Man turned back to John Doe and said, "I got a question, though. Your 'special guy.' What's that all about? What's his deal?"

"He started me on everything. See, I was an entirely

different person back then. I had been in reform school, and then in prison. I'd done a lot of bad shit. I *was* a piece of shit. My guy, he isn't a PO, or anything official. He's a free man. He's just this special guy, who people respect the hell out of. He connected with me. For some reason, he chose to help me, and completely changed my life for the better. Despite my past, he always said, 'There are no problems, only solutions.'"

John Doe continued. "He had lots of nicknames. The ones I liked best were 'Saint Kerry' or 'God Kerry', as in 'God Kerry works in mysterious ways.' Kerry has helped lots of people."

John Doe paused, looking around at the wide eyes and open mouths.

"What's up?" he said. "Am I talking too much? Did I say something wrong?"

Songbird covered her mouth with her hand. There was a continued awestruck moment among the group.

"They're all bloody gobsmacked!" observed Hoot.

Hoot's English-accented observation broke the stunned silence, and what followed was a deluge of questions about 'Carey' and 'Kerry.' Was it possible? It wasn't impossible. It couldn't be. But if it was, why? How?

John Doe, wary of any potential con, was cautious. But with Shredder's encouragement, he told what he knew about 'Kerry,' the man who had helped him. He slowly warmed to the possibility of a fantastic coincidence. Sir Lancelot outwardly lauded Carey / Kerry's selfless aid to others (while subconsciously pleased that Songbird liked his fable). Unicorn, of course, immediately latched on to the idea that the Carey / Kerry mystery was somehow related to the Angela Code and the commencement of realignment. Hoot was intrigued and watchful. Songbird, always wary and practical, was pleased to see Repo Man's delight. She thought he concealed melancholy under his "mellow dude" facade, and she was glad to see his happiness.

Repo Man had gratitude for them all. He was still good with the gray about the man he thought of as his 'uncle,' but he was unambiguously filled with love for his hiker companions, new and old.

• Epilogue •

The storytelling closeth. The hikers slept. At dawn the day next, so goeth the pilgrims on their way. Some hiking together; some alone; some hiking twenty miles or so; some hiking further. Shredder and John Doe did nearly forty. None took a zero day. The next night, new camps, different groups, and more tales. May God send every person help to ease their troubles.

Happy Trails! Amen.

The Pacific Crest Trail

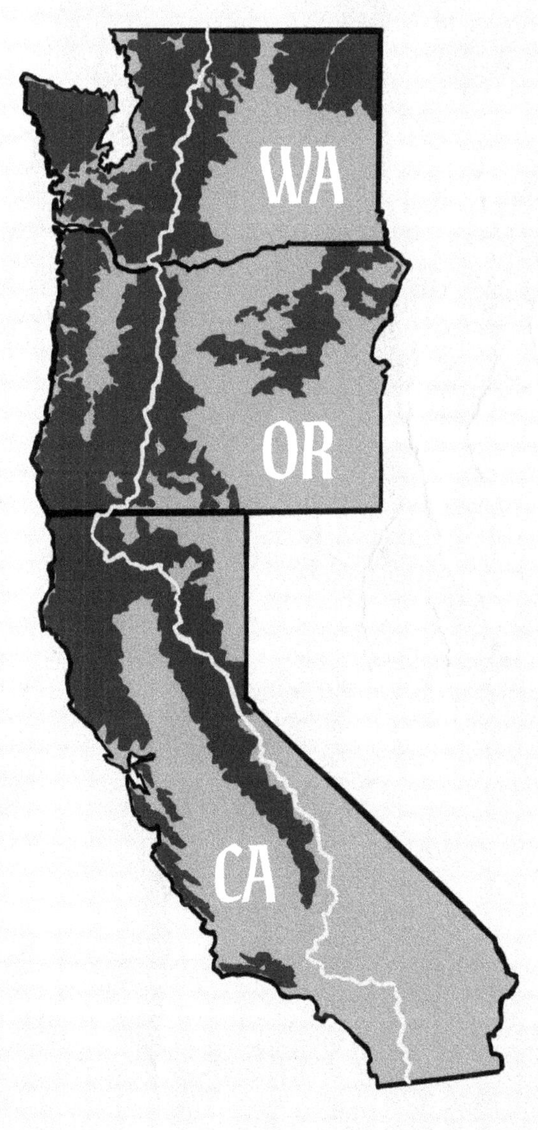

Hiking Glossary

AT: Appalachian Trail.

CD: Continental Divide Trail.

Katahdin: Northernmost terminus of the AT trail.

PCT: Pacific Crest Trail.

Through hiker: One who hikes all the way, or substantially all the way, from Mexico to Canada.

Trail family: Grouping of close friends met and fraternized with repeatedly along the trail.

Trail magic: Spontaneous gifts or treats or generous acts bestowed along the trail.

Trail name: Standard convention whereby hikers bestow nicknames (aliases) on other hikers. Proposed names can be rejected.

Twenty-four Hour Challenge: Hike for twenty-four hours straight.

Zero day: A day of rest in which the hiker does not hike any miles on the trail.